NOBODY LIKES MIKE HUNT

A PARODY BY

" JUNGLE" JACK STEELE

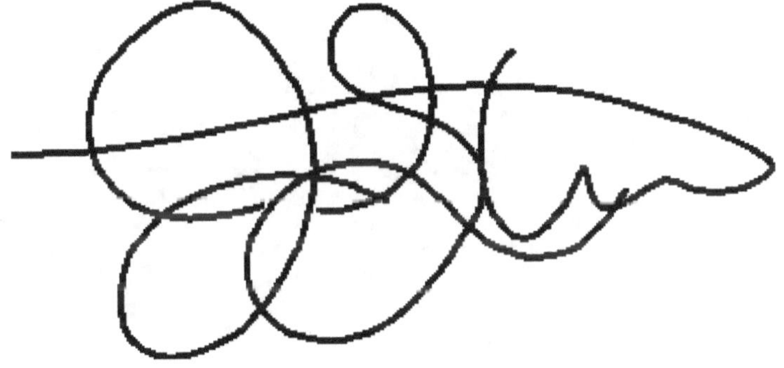

I have a boyfriend that's tall,

He can smell it all.

He asked "What's that funk"

It was Mike Hunt

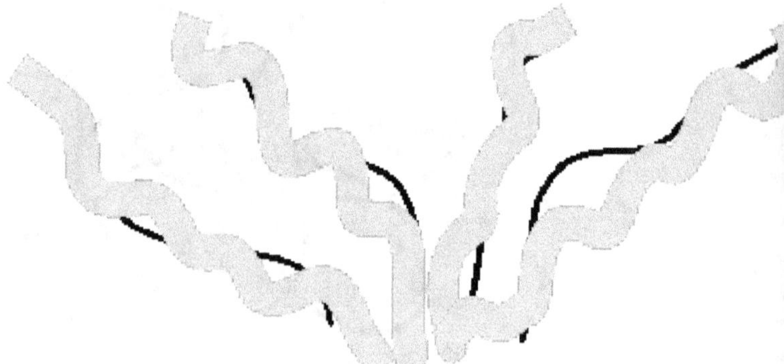

Mike Hunt is big,

Mike Hunt is hairy

And sometime Mike Hunt is

SCARY

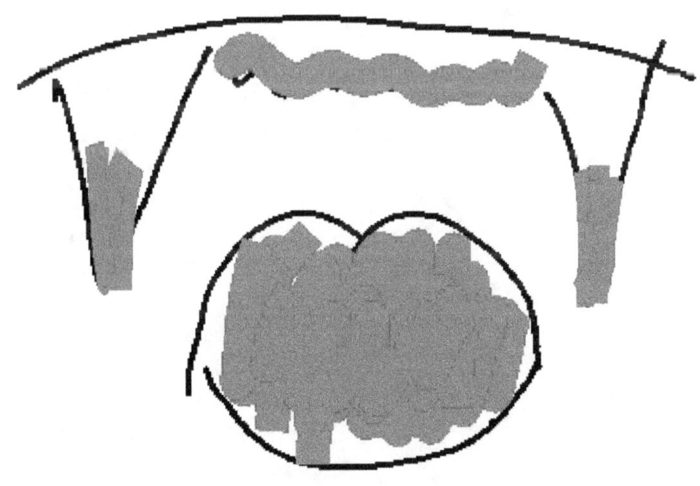

When Mike Hunt

Doesn't shave

He looks like madman

That misbehaves

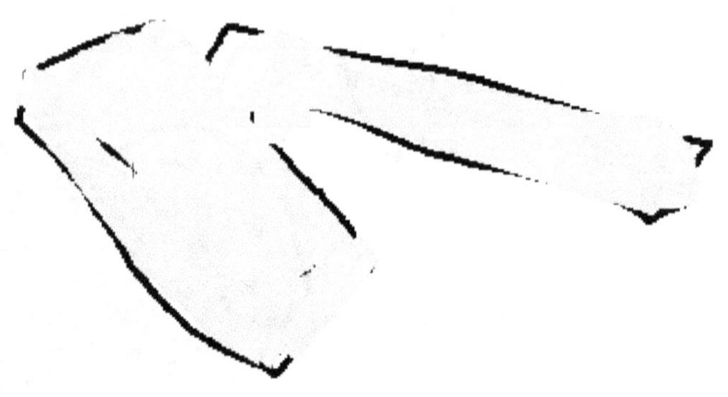

Mike Hunt loves food,

He wishes he was leaner

Mike Hunts favorite meal

Is huge wieners

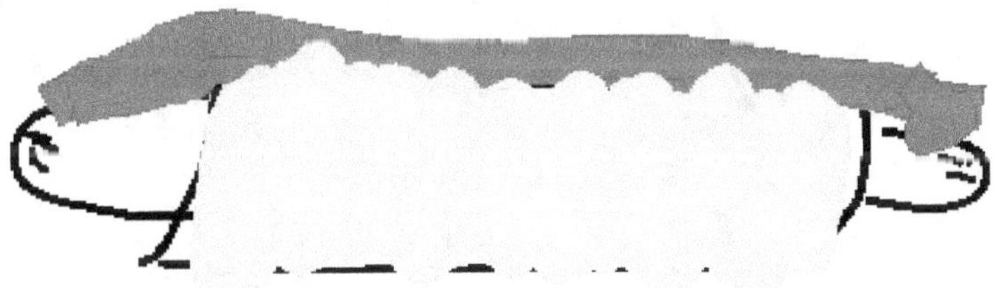

Mike Hunt loves cash

Some people say

Mike Hunt is trash

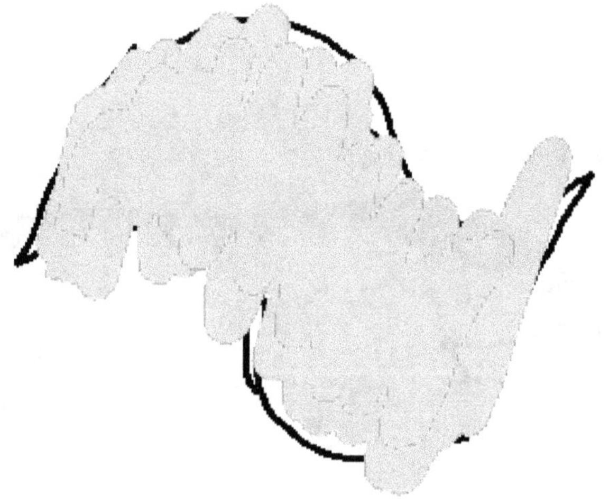

Mike Hunt hates lumps

But sometimes

Mike Hunt is covered in bumps

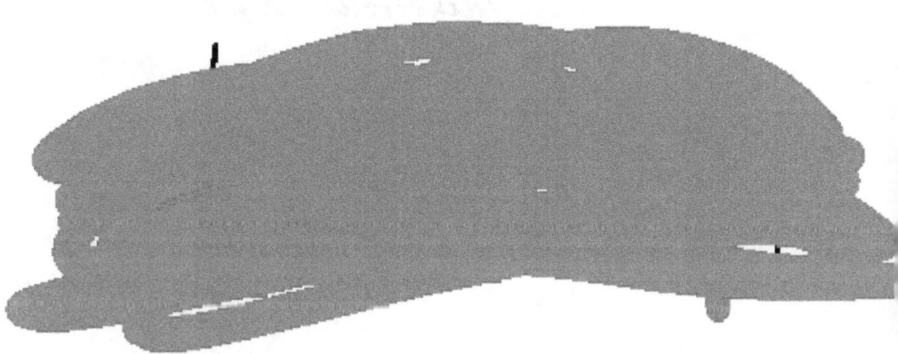

Mike Hunt gets loud

And well voiced

Sometimes at night

Mike Hunt is moist

People say they know

Before Mike Hunt shows

Because they follow their nose

Mike Hunt loves music

It makes him howl

If you listen close

Mike Hunt will growl

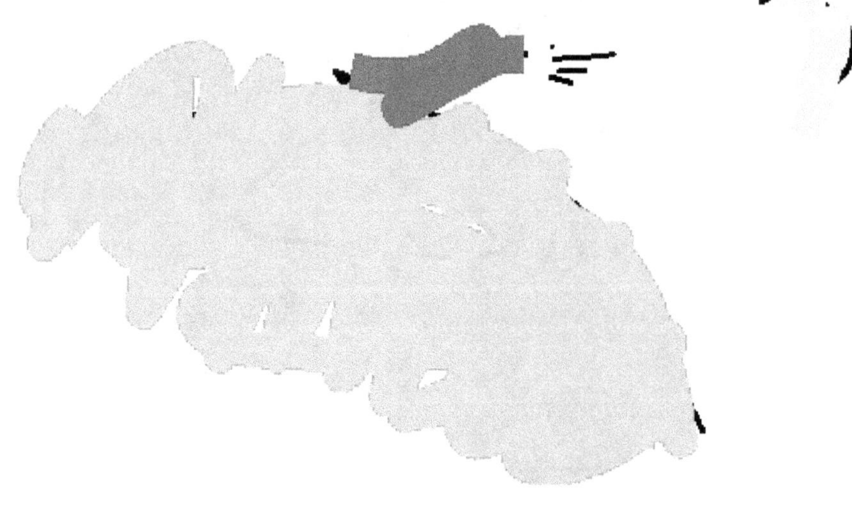

Mike Hunt loves men

Mike Hunt think it's a win

When he has 2 or 3 in

Mike Hunt is easy

Mike Hunt is fun

Mike Hunt is happy

When your done

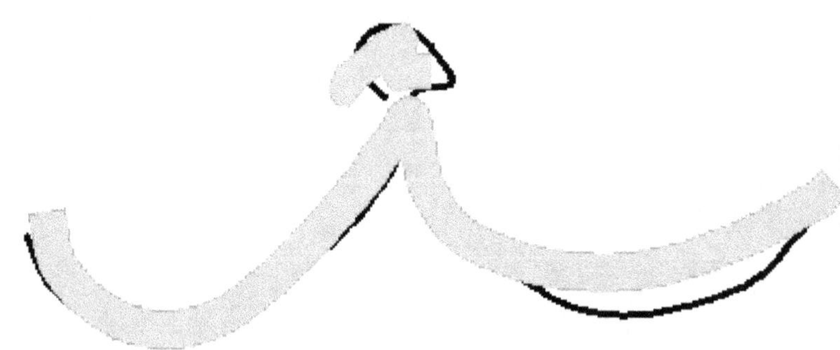

Mike Hunt seems to be hollow

Because all the impressive

Things he can swallow

Mike Hunt is alone

When he has

To pet himself on his own

Mike Hunt is fast

Mike Hunt is eager

No silly goose

He isn't a beaver

Mike Hunt likes poodles

Mike Hunt loves noodles

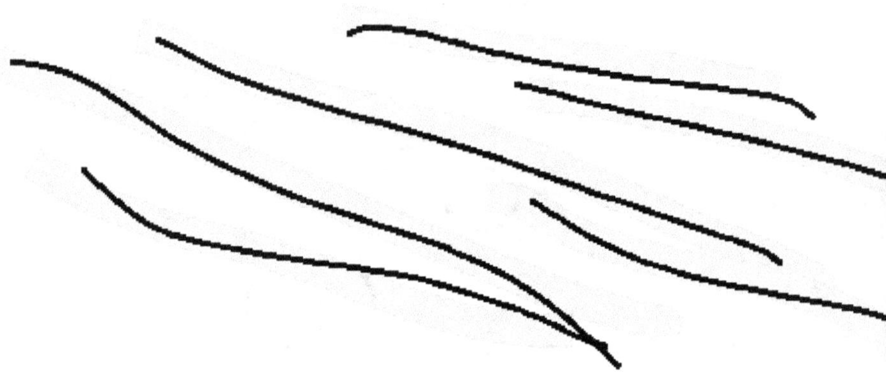

Mike Hunt is a mystery

What kind of thing could

Mike Hunt be?

Mike Hunt loves hills

Mike Hunt brings thrills

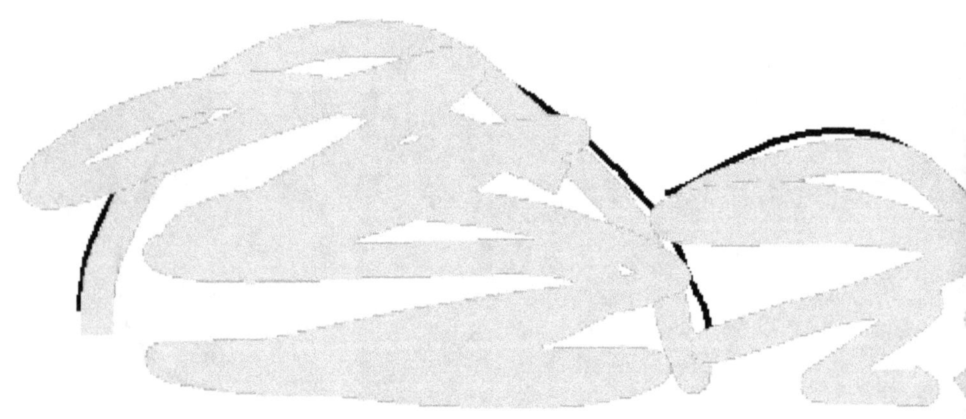

Mike Hunt loves

to get treats

Mike Hunt loves

To get meats

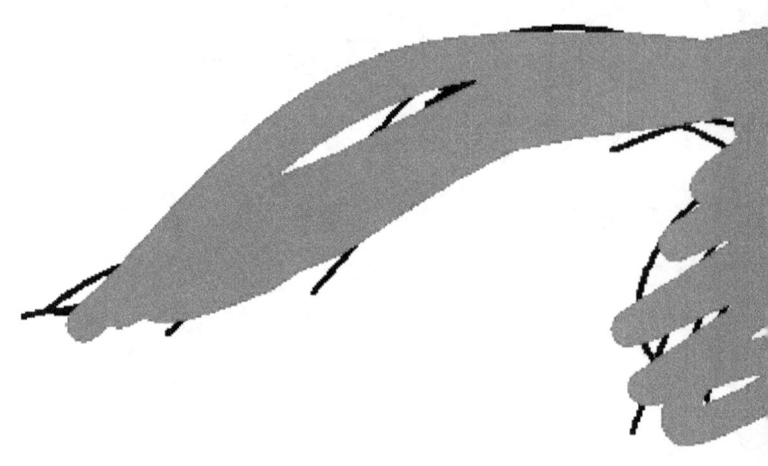

Do you know what Mike Hunt is?

Can you tell me where

Mike Hunt has been

Your right Mike Hunt is...

A Kitty Cat

Thanks for reading guys

This book is dedicated to Mike Hunt's of the world!

You have no idea how many times you've brought joy to someones day

Whether you knew it or not!

Book 2 in the Adult Childrens Book series

Check out "Your new friend Mr. Hangover"

A special thanks to Renee! This has been a fun ride and I hope it goes another 100 years!

You're the reason my fun is so enjoyable!

Thanks!